45 P

The Young World Library is a series designed for the
young reader. The stories are taken from some of the
world's best-known novels, plays, legends, operas and
ballets. They have been simplified and re-told in a way
which keeps close to the spirit of the original, while bringing
everything within the immediate grasp of the young
reader's understanding of words. Equally important are
the illustrations, which have been chosen both to delight
the eye and to match the special character of each story.
Thus the Young World Library offers young readers a
unique stepping stone towards the use and enjoyment of
books. It also introduces them in a lively, up-to-date way
to many famous stories and characters from the
wonderful world of literature and the performing arts.

Series Editor: Alan Blackwood

© 1974 Thomas Nelson & Sons Limited
SBN 72381026 5
Printed in Great Britain by A. Wheaton & Co., Exeter.

MAX AND THE MAGIC BULLETS

Adapted and told by
Alan Blackwood

Illustrated by
Christine Skilton

Based on the opera *Der Freischütz* by
Carl Maria von Weber

**NELSON
YOUNG WORLD**

Max was a handsome young
woodsman. During the day
he worked in the forest.

In the evenings he drank
wine in the village inn and
sang songs with his friends.
He should have been the
happiest young man in the
world.

But Max was worried and unhappy. He was in love with Agatha. She was the daughter of Prince Ottokar. She was beautiful, but she was proud as well.

"I shall marry the man who wins the shooting contest," she declared. "Only the most skilful marksman is good enough for me."

Max was worried in case he did not win the contest. Then he would never gain Agatha's hand in marriage.

"I can use an axe better than anyone," he told his friend Caspar. "You've seen how quickly and cleanly I can cut down a tree. But I'm not so skilled with a gun. And it's too late to practise now. The contest is being held tomorrow."

Caspar gave Max his own gun. "See that eagle up there in the sky?" he asked. "Shoot it."

"I couldn't possibly hit something as far away as that," Max replied.

"Do as I say," Caspar urged. "Just aim the gun and fire."

11

So Max did as he was told. To his amazement, the eagle fell to the ground at his feet.

"I can't believe it!" he exclaimed. "The gun seemed to take aim and fire as though by magic!"

Caspar laughed. "Magic indeed, Max," he said. "But not a magic gun. It was the bullet you fired which was magic."

Caspar told Max that his bullets
were made for him by the Devil.

"One day, when I was walking
near the Wolf's Glen, the Devil
spoke to me," Caspar said. "He
offered to make these magic
bullets. With bullets like these
you can hit any target you wish."

"Listen Max. Tonight is the night of the full moon. The Devil is sure to be at the Wolf's Glen. Come with me, and I'll ask him to give you some magic bullets. Then you'll win the shooting contest tomorrow, and Agatha shall be your bride."

Max was scared. The Wolf's Glen
was a bleak and lonely place up
in the mountains. He had been
told it was the meeting place
of witches, vampires, demons,
and other evil creatures. Few
people ever went near the Wolf's
Glen, even in daytime. To go
there at night was asking for
trouble.

But he loved Agatha. He
wanted, more than anything, to
win the shooting contest, and
so win her proud heart.

"Alright," he said to Caspar.
"I'll come with you to the Wolf's
Glen."

It was getting dark as Max
and Caspar set out through the
forest for the Wolf's Glen.
There were clouds in the sky.

"Perhaps the moon won't
shine tonight," Max said.
"What happens then? Does the
Devil only go to the Wolf's
Glen when the full moon shines?"

"Wait and see," Caspar told
him. "The Devil will do
whatever he wishes."

As Max and Caspar drew near to
the Wolf's Glen, they could hear
the wolves howling.

"The wolves are crying for the
moon," Caspar said. "When the
moon comes out they will start
hunting. Pity the poor animals
of the forest that are hunted by
the wolves on such a night!"

"This is the place," Caspar whispered to Max.

In the darkness Max could just make out a great rocky cliff, towering above them.

Then, all at once, the clouds drifted apart. The full moon lit the scene with a ghostly, silvery light.

Max could see, at the foot of the cliff, a circle of rocks and stones. He could also see the bones of animals which the wolves had eaten. And in the middle of the circle he could see a large cauldron.

23

Suddenly there was a flash of
lightning, and a terrific crash
of thunder. Max nearly jumped
out of his skin.

"Welcome, my dear Caspar,"
said a voice which echoed round
the Wolf's Glen.

Max jumped again. He couldn't
see anyone, but he realised it
must be the Devil himself who
was speaking.

"Who is this young man?" the Devil asked Caspar. "What does he want?"

"This is Max, Oh Master," Caspar replied. "He wants some of your magic bullets, so that he may win the shooting contest in our village."

"So Max," the Devil said. "You want some of my magic bullets too. Very well. I shall give you seven bullets. Six of them shall hit any target you wish. The seventh shall hit a target of my choice. Agreed?"

Max swallowed hard, and nodded his head.

"Then let us begin," the Devil said. "I shall cast the bullets in my cauldron."

27

The cauldron began to boil and
bubble, and smoke and steam rose
from it in a thick cloud. Then,
as the Devil cast each bullet,
a wind began to blow. It was
like a whirlwind. It blew
faster and faster round the
cauldron. It sounded like the
screaming of demons. Max thought
he could see their horrible faces
swirling round and round the
cauldron.

   He felt dizzy. His legs felt
weak. He fell to the ground in
a faint.

When Max opened his eyes again,
he was back in his own house.
He was lying on his bed. The
sun was shining through the
windows. Caspar was standing
there.

"Wake up, Max!" he said.
"You're a fine one, I must say!
I had to carry you all the way
back from the Wolf's Glen.
Now, here are your seven magic
bullets. It's the shooting
contest today. You'd better
get ready."

Max shuddered when he remembered the scene at the Wolf's Glen. He wished he'd never gone there. Still, he did have the magic bullets. And if Caspar spoke the truth, then he must win the contest.

So he got up, put the bullets in his pocket, and picked up his gun. Then he set out for Prince Ottokar's castle, where the contest was to be held.

There was a large crowd in the castle courtyard. People had come from many miles to see the contest. Prince Ottokar was going to judge the event. He sat upon his throne. Next to him sat his beautiful daughter, Agatha.

"Let the contest begin," the prince declared. "Whoever wins may claim my daughter for his bride."

34

It was Max's turn to fire. He noticed Caspar standing alone up on the battlements, watching him. Would something terrible happen as soon as he fired one of the magic bullets?

It was too late to worry about
that now. He placed the first of
the bullets in his gun, took a
deep breath, aimed at the target,
and fired.

He hit the bullseye every time.

"Well done, Max," Prince Ottokar said. "You have won the contest. Indeed, I have heard already about your skills as a marksman. I am told that only yesterday you shot an eagle. Look, there is another eagle high up in the sky. Shoot that one specially for me."

Max loaded his gun with another
of his magic bullets. It was
the last one. The seventh
bullet. The one which the
Devil had claimed for himself!
Max's hand trembled as he raised
his gun and took aim. What would
happen this time?

He pulled the trigger and fired. The eagle did not fall from the sky. Instead, there was a cry from the battlements. It was Caspar. He fell from the battlements into the waters of the moat. He was the target for the Devil's seventh magic bullet!

The crowds cheered Max as he
left the castle with Agatha.
She had promised to be his
bride. But as Max crossed the
drawbridge, he saw some soldiers
by the moat. They were dragging
Caspar's dead body out of the
water. That's what came of
meddling with the Devil and
his evil powers.

Max felt lucky still to be alive. He
swore that he would never,
never go near the Wolf's Glen
again.